DOCTOR KISS SAYS YES

Canadian Cataloguing in Publication Data

Jam, Teddy
Dr. Kiss says yes

ISBN 0-88899-141-X

I. Fitzgerald, Joanne, 1956-   .   II. Title.

PS8569.A52D7 1991   jC813'.54   C91-093790-7
PZ7.J35Dr 1991

A Groundwood Book
Douglas & McIntyre
585 Bloor Street West
Toronto, Ontario M6G 1K5

Design by Michael Soloman
Printed and bound in Hong Kong
by Everbest Printing Co. Ltd.

DOCTOR KISS
SAYS YES

By Teddy Jam
Pictures by Joanne Fitzgerald

A Groundwood Book
Douglas & McIntyre
TORONTO/VANCOUVER

NE day after Doctor Kiss got home from school she found an envelope under her pillow. Inside the envelope were two cardboard squares and a letter.

Dear Doctor Kiss:

We need your help tonight.

Will you come?

x.

One cardboard square was red. The other was green.
Doctor Kiss read the letter and then she read it again.

"Yes!" said Doctor Kiss. She opened her doctor kit, took
out some tape, and taped the green square to the window.

"Are you hungry?" asked Doctor Kiss's mother at supper.
"Yes!" said Doctor Kiss, because she knew she would
have to be very strong tonight.

"Are you ready to go to your room?" asked Doctor Kiss's father when it was time for bed.

"Yes!" said Doctor Kiss, climbing onto her father's shoulders. She wanted to go to bed and get ready for her adventure.

"Do you want us to turn out your light?" asked Doctor Kiss's mother and father after they had read her a story, given her one million kisses, fifteen hugs, forty squeezes and five tickles for good luck.

Doctor Kiss's mother put on Doctor Kiss's favourite tape. Doctor Kiss's father brought Doctor Kiss one box of pineapple juice with a straw, one apple cut into eight pieces and her doctor kit.

"Goodnight Doctor Kiss," said Doctor Kiss's mother.

"Goodnight Doctor Kiss," said Doctor Kiss's father.

"Goodnight," said Doctor Kiss. "Please don't forget to close my door."

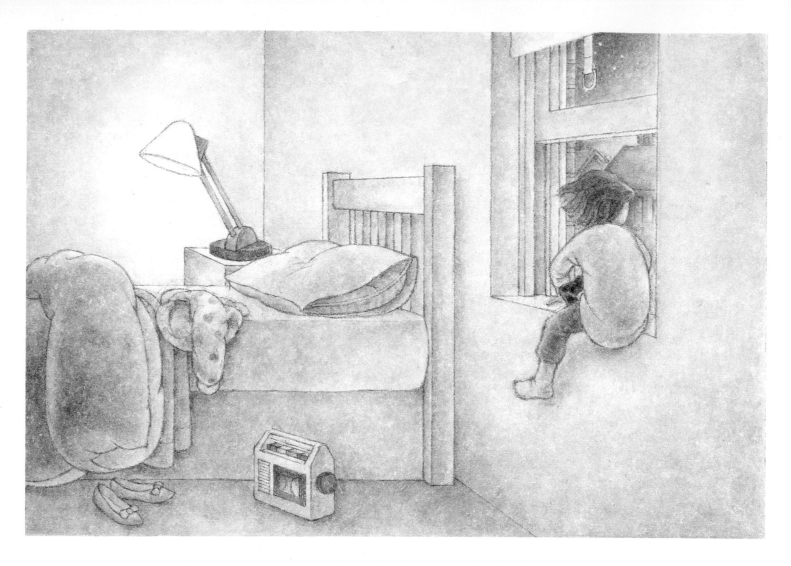

Doctor Kiss put on her clothes and climbed out the window.

At the edge of the forest a young squire was waiting for her with a horse. "Thank you for coming, Doctor Kiss. We saw your signal in the window. Would you like to ride this horse?"

"Yes!" said Doctor Kiss.

They galloped through the forest. Doctor Kiss felt the
moonlight and the wind against her face.

They rode until they came to a small clearing. In the middle was a tall tent.

"Here we are," said the squire.

Inside the tent, lying on cushions and blankets, was a knight. His weapons and armour were piled beside him. Kneeling and holding his hand was a beautiful lady with long hair.

"Oh Doctor Kiss!" cried the damsel. "Can you help this poor broken knight?"

"I hope so," said Doctor Kiss. "What is the matter?"

The damsel began to weep. The squire turned away because he did not want anyone to see him cry. "This afternoon there was a terrible battle.

My brave knight and his friends were riding through the forest singing songs. Then they were attacked by evil knights riding giant black horses."

"How terrible," said Doctor Kiss.

"They fought for hours, crashing their swords against each other and roaring like lions."

"What an enormous noise," said Doctor Kiss.

"Sir Roderick charged three of the black knights at once."
"How brave," said Doctor Kiss.

"Sir Gawain fought with his cat on his shoulder."
"How unusual," said Doctor Kiss.

"When Sir Gawain was knocked from his horse, my Roderick gathered up Gawain and his cat and rode them to safety."

"How gallant," said Doctor Kiss.

"Now Sir Gawain is home with his mother."

"And Roderick?"

"Here. Beneath these blankets. Growing ever weaker."

"What happened to him?" asked Doctor Kiss.

"He scraped his knees and now they are extremely sore."

Doctor Kiss leaned over the knight's knees and looked at them.

"They both hurt," declared Sir Roderick. "Mighty thumps did they receive as the giant black horses crashed against them. Once, twice, a thousand times I was squeezed between those beasts. Can you make them better?"

"Yes!" said Doctor Kiss. She took a box out of her doctor kit and opened it up. "This is one of my secrets," she said. Then she found two big bandages and put them on his knees.

"Are they all better?"

"Yes!" said Doctor Kiss.

"But they still hurt."

"Well then," said Doctor Kiss, "count to a thousand and then go to sleep. In the morning you will be a new knight."

"I still can't sleep," said Sir Roderick. "I need one million kisses, fifteen hugs, forty squeezes and five tickles for good luck. Also, if you don't mind, one box of pineapple juice with a straw and one apple cut into eight pieces."

"All right," said Doctor Kiss.

Doctor Kiss left the tent. The moon was above her in the sky. It shone down on the knight's mysterious tent and made little moons in the eyes of the horse that was waiting to carry her home.

At breakfast Doctor Kiss's mother asked if she had slept
well.

"Yes!" said Doctor Kiss.

"Are you hungry?" asked her father.

"Yes!" said Doctor Kiss. "Very."